"AFTER YOU"

by Janet Riehecky
illustrated by Gwen Connelly

Created by

THE
CHILD'S
WORLD

Distributed by CHILDRENS PRESS®
Chicago, Illinois

CHILDRENS PRESS HARDCOVER EDITION
ISBN 0-516-06235-2

CHILDRENS PRESS PAPERBACK EDITION
ISBN 0-516-46235-0

Library of Congress Cataloging in Publication Data

Riehecky, Janet, 1953-
   "After you" / by Janet Riehecky ; illustrated by Gwen Connelly.
    p. cm. — (Manners matter)
   Summary: Describes various situations in which it is appropriate
to say, "After you."
   ISBN 0-89565-538-1. — ISBN 0-89565-540-3 (pbk.)
   1. Etiquette for children and youth.   [1. Etiquette.]
I. Connelly, Gwen, ill.   II. Title.   III. Series: Riehecky, Janet,
1953- Manners matter.
BJ1857.C5R46   1989
395'.122—dc20   89-31606
                                    CIP
                                      AC

1 2 3 4 5 6 7 8 9 10 11 12 R 97 96 95 94 93 92 91 90 89

"AFTER YOU"

MANNERS MATTER all day through.
Say, "I'm sorry" or "I didn't mean to."

"Please" or "May I?" or "After you"
Will help you with what you want to do.

When you treat others with respect and care,
You'll find you have friends everywhere.

4

Say "After you" and not "Me first,"
or you might . . .

knock someone over . . .

Say "after you" and not "me first" or you might...

break the doll . . .

Say "after you" and not "me first" or you might...

get in a fight . . .

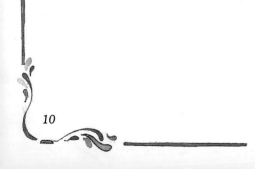

Say "after you" and not "me first" or you might...

not fit . . .

Say "after you" and not "me first" or you might...

crash . . .

make everything fall . . .

Say "after you" and not "me first" or you might...

end up on the ground . . .

Say "after you" and not "me first" or you might...

hurt your friend's feelings . . .

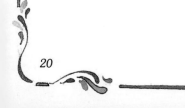

Say "after you" and not "me first" or you might...

spill the paint . . .

rip the pages . . .

Say "after you" and not "me first" or you might...

make a mess . . .

Say "after you" and not "me first" or you might...

spill the neighbor's groceries . . .

never get anywhere.

When you say "After you" and let someone else go first, you show consideration for others—and you avoid trouble.